**Put Beginning Readers on the Right Track with
ALL ABOARD READING™**

The All Aboard Reading series is especially designed for beginning readers. Written by noted authors and illustrated in full color, these are books that children really want to read—books to excite their imagination, expand their interests, make them laugh, and support their feelings. With fiction and nonfiction stories that are high interest and curriculum-related, All Aboard Reading books offer something for every young reader. And with four different reading levels, the All Aboard Reading series lets you choose which books are most appropriate for your children and their growing abilities.

Picture Readers
Picture Readers have super-simple texts, with many nouns appearing as rebus pictures. At the end of each book are 24 flash cards—on one side is a rebus picture; on the other side is the written-out word.

Station Stop 1
Station Stop 1 books are best for children who have just begun to read. Simple words and big type make these early reading experiences more comfortable. Picture clues help children to figure out the words on the page. Lots of repetition throughout the text helps children to predict the next word or phrase—an essential step in developing word recognition.

Station Stop 2
Station Stop 2 books are written specifically for children who are reading with help. Short sentences make it easier for early readers to understand what they are reading. Simple plots and simple dialogue help children with reading comprehension.

Station Stop 3
Station Stop 3 books are perfect for children who are reading alone. With longer text and harder words, these books appeal to children who have mastered basic reading skills. More complex stories captivate children who are ready for more challenging books.

In addition to All Aboard Reading books, look for All Aboard Math Readers™ (fiction stories that teach math concepts children are learning in school); All Aboard Science Readers™ (nonfiction books that explore the most fascinating science topics in age-appropriate language); All Aboard Poetry Readers™ (funny, rhyming poems for readers of all levels); and All Aboard Mystery Readers™ (puzzling tales where children piece together evidence with the characters).

All Aboard for happy reading!

Cotton	Feathers	Freddie Frog	Lollichop	Maxwell Mouse	Sally Squirrel	Terrence Turtle

GROSSET & DUNLAP
Published by the Penguin Group
Penguin Group (USA) Inc., 375 Hudson Street, New York, New York 10014, U.S.A.
Penguin Group (Canada), 90 Eglinton Avenue East, Suite 700, Toronto, Ontario, Canada M4P 2Y3
(a division of Pearson Penguin Canada Inc.)
Penguin Books Ltd, 80 Strand, London WC2R 0RL, England
Penguin Ireland, 25 St Stephen's Green, Dublin 2, Ireland
(a division of Penguin Books Ltd)
Penguin Group (Australia), 250 Camberwell Road, Camberwell, Victoria 3124, Australia
(a division of Pearson Australia Group Pty Ltd)
Penguin Books India Pvt Ltd, 11 Community Centre, Panchsheel Park, New Delhi - 110 017, India
Penguin Group (NZ), Cnr Airborne and Rosedale Roads, Albany, Auckland 1310, New Zealand
(a division of Pearson New Zealand Ltd)
Penguin Books (South Africa) (Pty) Ltd, 24 Sturdee Avenue, Rosebank, Johannesburg 2196, South Africa

Penguin Books Ltd, Registered Offices:
80 Strand, London WC2R 0RL, England

ISBN 978-0-448-44488-8   10 9 8 7 6 5 4 3 2 1

PAAS®

The Easter Egg Hunt

By Ann Bryant
Illustrated by Artful Doodlers

Grosset & Dunlap

It is almost time for the

Easter  hunt!

's pals come over

to his house.

"Hi, everybody!"  says.

"Let's go look for

Easter !"

The pals skip

down the path.

 stops at the

patch.

He sees an .

And an  Easter  !

Good job,  !

Put it in your .

 sees a group

of  .

She sees something else

that is :

an Easter  !

Good job, !

Put it in your .

 looks at the .

They are bright .

Something is hiding

in the .

It is a  Easter !

Good job, !

Put it in your .

hops among

the .

They smell so nice.

What's that?

It's a !

Good job, !

Put it in your .

 sees a .

She wants to play with it.

Then she sees

something else:

a  Easter !

Good job, !

Put it in your .

 goes down

to the  .

He likes to splash around.

What's that in the 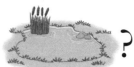 ?

It is a  Easter !

Good job, !

Put it in your .

All of the pals found

an Easter ,

except for .

"My  is empty!"

"Don't cry, !"

 says.

"You just have

to keep looking."

 gives  a hug.

"Thank you," he says.

 looks up at a .

"Look!"  yells.

"I found an !"

But the is so high

and is very small.

How will he get it down?

 and  stand

at the bottom of the .

 and  climb

on their backs.

 and  hop on top.

Now can reach.

Good job, !

Put the  in your  .

After the hunt, the pals

play on the  .

They found so many

Easter  today!

Happy Easter, everybody!

Cotton	egg
eggs	carrot
orange	basket

Lollichop	yellow
chicks	Terrence Turtle
bushes	green

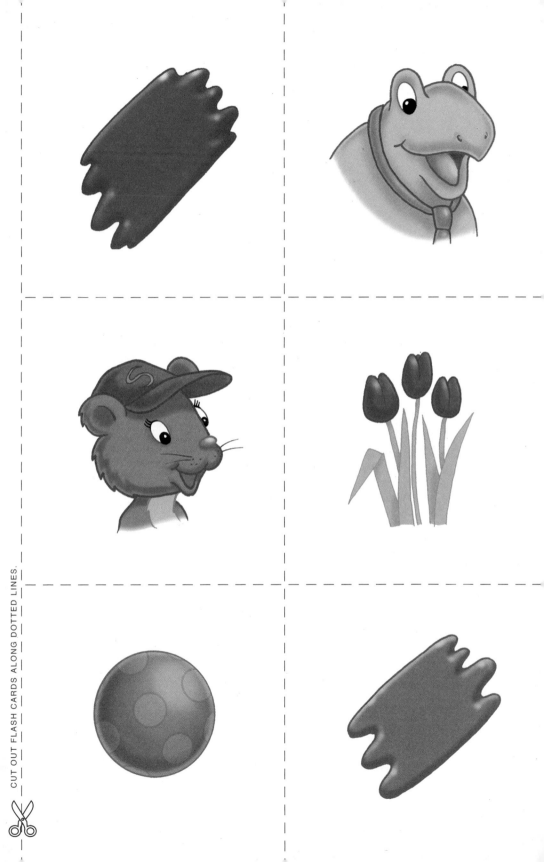

Freddie Frog	red
flowers	Sally Squirrel
purple	ball

Feathers	pond
blue	Maxwell Mouse
tree	grass